Andrew Lang

XXXII Ballades in Blue China

Andrew Lang

XXXII Ballades in Blue China

ISBN/EAN: 9783744780032

Printed in Europe, USA, Canada, Australia, Japan

Cover: Foto ©Andreas Hilbeck / pixelio.de

More available books at **www.hansebooks.com**

A. LANG

XXXII Ballades

in Blue China

Tout   Scalles

par

LONDON

KEGAN PAUL, TRENCH & CO

MDCCCLXXXVIII

A BALLADE OF XXXII BALLADES.

Friend, when you bear a care-dulled eye,
And brow perplexed with things of weight,
And fain would bid some charm untie
The bonds that hold you all too strait,
Behold a solace to your fate,
Wrapped in this cover's china blue ;
These ballades fresh and delicate,
This dainty troop of Thirty-two !

The mind, unwearied, longs to fly
And commune with the wise and great ;
But that same ether, rare and high,
Which glorifies its worthy mate,
To breath forspent is disparate :
Laughing and light and airy-new
These come to tickle the dull pate,
This dainty troop of Thirty-two.

A BALLADE.

Most welcome then, when you and I,
Forestalling days for mirth too late,
To quips and cranks and fantasy
Some choice half-hour dedicate,
They weave their dance with measured rate
Of rhymes enlinked in order due,
Till frowns relax and cares abate,
This dainty troop of Thirty-two.

ENVOY.

Princes, of toys that please your state
Quainter are surely none to view
Than these which pass with tripping gait,
This dainty troop of Thirty-two.

F. P.

TO

AUSTIN DOBSON.

Un Livre est un ami
qui change—quelquefois.

1880
—
1888

a

The Verses which did not appear in the original edition of *Ballades in Blue China* have for the most part been published in Longman's and Harper's Magazines.

CONTENTS.

VERSES AND TRANSLATIONS.

BALLADE TO THEOCRITUS, IN WINTER.

ἐσορῶν τὰν Σικελὰν ἐς ἅλα.

Id. viii. 56.

Ah ! leave the smoke, the wealth, the roar
Of London, and the bustling street,
For still, by the Sicilian shore,
The murmur of the Muse is sweet.
Still, still, the suns of summer greet
The mountain-grave of Helikê,
And shepherds still their songs repeat
Where breaks the blue Sicilian sea.

What though they worship Pan no more,
That guarded once the shepherd's seat,
They chatter of their rustic lore,
They watch the wind among the wheat:

Cicalas chirp, the young lambs bleat,
Where whispers pine to cypress tree ;
They count the waves that idly beat
Where breaks the blue Sicilian sea.

Theocritus ! thou canst restore
The pleasant years, and over-fleet ;
With thee we live as men of yore,
We rest where running waters meet :
And then we turn unwilling feet
And seek the world—so must it be—
We may not linger in the heat
Where breaks the blue Sicilian sea !

ENVOY.

Master,—when rain, and snow, and sleet
And northern winds are wild, to thee
We come, we rest in thy retreat,
Where breaks the blue Sicilian sea !

BALLADE OF CLEOPATRA'S NEEDLE.

Ye giant shades of RA and TUM,
Ye ghosts of gods Egyptian,
If murmurs of our planet come
To exiles in the precincts wan
Where, fetish or Olympian,
To help or harm no more ye list,
Look down, if look ye may, and scan
This monument in London mist!

Behold, the hieroglyphs are dumb
That once were read of him that ran
When seistron, cymbal, trump, and drum
Wild music of the Bull began ;
When through the chanting priestly clan
Walk'd Ramses, and the high sun kiss'd
This stone, with blessing scored and ban—
This monument in London mist.

The stone endures though gods be numb;
Though human effort, plot, and plan
Be sifted, drifted, like the sum
Of sands in wastes Arabian.
What king may deem him more than man,
What priest says Faith can Time resist
While *this* endures to mark their span—
This monument in London mist?

ENVOY.

Prince, the stone's shade on your divan
Falls; it is longer than ye wist:
It preaches, as Time's gnomon can,
This monument in London mist!

BALLADE OF ROULETTE.

TO R. R.

This life—one was thinking to-day,
In the midst of a medley of fancies—
Is a game, and the board where we play
Green earth with her poppies and pansies.
Let *manque* be faded romances,
Be *passe* remorse and regret ;
Hearts dance with the wheel as it dances—
The wheel of Dame Fortune's roulette.

The lover will stake as he may
His heart on his Peggies and Nancies ;
The girl has her beauty to lay ;
The saint has his prayers and his trances ;
The poet bets endless expanses
In Dreamland ; the scamp has his debt :
How they gaze at the wheel as it glances—
The wheel of Dame Fortune's roulette !

The Kaiser will stake his array
Of sabres, of Krupps, and of lances
An Englishman punts with his pay,
And glory the *jeton* of France is ;
Your artists, or Whistlers or Vances,
Have voices or colours to bet ;
Will you moan that its motion askance is—
The wheel of Dame Fortune's roulette ?

ENVOY.

The prize that the pleasure enhances?
The prize is—at last to forget
The changes, the chops, and the chances—
The wheel of Dame Fortune's roulette.

BALLADE OF SLEEP.

The hours are passing slow,
I hear their weary tread
Clang from the tower, and go
Back to their kinsfolk dead.
Sleep ! death's twin brother dread !
Why dost thou scorn me so ?
The wind's voice overhead
Long wakeful here I know,
And music from the steep
Where waters fall and flow.
Wilt thou not hear me, Sleep ?

All sounds that might bestow
Rest on the fever'd bed,
All slumb'rous sounds and low
Are mingled here and wed,
And bring no drowsihed.

Shy dreams flit to and fro
With shadowy hair dispread ;
With wistful eyes that glow,
And silent robes that sweep.
Thou wilt not hear me ; no ?
Wilt thou not hear me, Sleep ?

What cause hast thou to show
Of sacrifice unsped ?
Of all thy slaves below
I most have labourèd
With service sung and said ;
Have cull'd such buds as blow,
Soft poppies white and red,
Where thy still gardens grow,
And Lethe's waters weep.
Why, then, art thou my foe ?
Wilt thou not hear me, Sleep ?

ENVOY.

Prince, ere the dark be shred
By golden shafts, ere low

And long the shadows creep :
Lord of the wand of lead,
Soft-footed as the snow,
Wilt thou not hear me, Sleep !

BALLADE OF THE MIDNIGHT FOREST.

AFTER THÉODORE DE BANVILLE.

Still sing the mocking fairies, as of old,
Beneath the shade of thorn and holly-tree ;
The west wind breathes upon them, pure and
      cold,
And wolves still dread Diana roaming free
In secret woodland with her company.
'Tis thought the peasants' hovels know her
      rite
When now the wolds are bathed in silver
      light,
And first the moonrise breaks the dusky grey,
Then down the dells, with blown soft hair and
      bright,
And through the dim wood Dian threads her
      way.

With water-weeds twined in their locks of
     gold
The strange cold forest-fairies dance in glee,
Sylphs over-timorous and over-bold
Haunt the dark hollows where the dwarf may be
The wild red dwarf, the nixies' enemy ;
Then 'mid their mirth, and laughter, and
      affright,
The sudden Goddess enters, tall and white,
With one long sigh for summers pass'd away ;
The swift feet tear the ivy nets outright
And through the dim wood Dian threads her way.

She gleans her silvan trophies ; down the wold
She hears the sobbing of the stags that flee
Mixed with the music of the hunting roll'd,
But her delight is all in archery,
And naught of ruth and pity wotteth she
More than her hounds that follow on the flight ;
The goddess draws a golden bow of might
And thick she rains the gentle shafts that slay.
She tosses loose her locks upon the night,
And through the dim wood Dian threads her way.

ENVOY.

Prince, let us leave the din, the dust, the spite,
The gloom and glare of towns, the plague, the
    blight :
Amid the forest leaves and fountain spray
There is the mystic home of our delight,
And through the dim wood Dian threads her
    way.

BALLADE OF THE TWEED.

(LOWLAND SCOTCH.)

TO T. W. LANG.

The ferox rins in rough Loch Awe,
A weary cry frae ony toun ;
The Spey, that loups o'er linn and fa',
They praise a' ither streams aboon ;
They boast their braes o' bonny Doon :
Gie *me* to hear the ringing reel,
Where shilfas sing, and cushats croon
By fair Tweed-side, at Ashiesteel !

There's Ettrick, Meggat, Ail, and a',
Where trout swim thick in May and June ;
Ye'll see them take in showers o' snaw
Some blinking, cauldrife April noon :
Rax ower the palmer and march-broun,
And syne we'll show a bonny creel,
In spring or simmer, late or soon,
By fair Tweed-side, at Ashiesteel !

There's mony a water, great or sma',
Gaes singing in his siller tune,
Through glen and heugh, and hope and shaw,
Beneath the sun-licht or the moon :
But set us in our fishing-shoon
Between the Caddon-burn and Peel,
And syne we'll cross the heather broun
By fair Tweed-side at Ashiesteel !

ENVOY.

Deil take the dirty, trading loon
Wad gar the water ca' his wheel,
And drift his dyes and poisons doun
By fair Tweed-side at Ashiesteel !

BALLADE OF THE BOOK-HUNTER.

In torrid heats of late July,
In March, beneath the bitter *bise*,
He book-hunts while the loungers fly,—
He book-hunts, though December freeze ;
In breeches baggy at the knees,
And heedless of the public jeers,
For these, for these, he hoards his fees,—
Aldines, Bodonis, Elzevirs.

No dismal stall escapes his eye,
He turns o'er tomes of low degrees,
There soiled romanticists may lie,
Or Restoration comedies ;
Each tract that flutters in the breeze
For him is charged with hopes and fears,
In mouldy novels fancy sees
Aldines, Bodonis, Elzevirs.

With restless eyes that peer and spy,
Sad eyes that heed not skies nor trees,
In dismal nooks he loves to pry,
Whose motto evermore is *Spes!*
But ah ! the fabled treasure flees ;
Grown rarer with the fleeting years,
In rich men's shelves they take their ease,—
Aldines, Bodonis, Elzevirs !

ENVOY.

Prince, all the things that tease and please,—
Fame, hope, wealth, kisses, cheers, and tears,
What are they but such toys as these—
Aldines, Bodonis, Elzevirs ?

BALLADE OF THE VOYAGE TO CYTHERA.

AFTER THÉODORE DE BANVILLE.

I know Cythera long is desolate ;
I know the winds have stripp'd the gardens
    green.
Alas, my friends ! beneath the fierce sun's
    weight
A barren reef lies where Love's flowers have
    been,
Nor ever lover on that coast is seen !
So be it, but we seek a fabled shore,
To lull our vague desires with mystic lore,
To wander where Love's labyrinths beguile ;
There let us land, there dream for evermore :
" It may be we shall touch the happy isle."

The sea may be our sepulchre.   If Fate,
If tempests wreak their wrath on us, serene
We watch the bolt of heaven, and scorn the hate
Of angry gods that smite us in their spleen.
Perchance the jealous mists are but the screen
That veils the fairy coast we would explore.
Come, though the sea be vex'd, and breakers
     roar,
Come, for the air of this old world is vile,
Haste we, and toil, and faint not at the oar ;
"It may be we shall touch the happy isle."

Grey serpents trail in temples desecrate
Where Cypris smiled, the golden maid, the queen,
And ruined is the palace of our state ;
But happy Loves flit round the mast, and keen
The shrill wind sings the silken cords between.
Heroes are we, with wearied hearts and sore,
Whose flower is faded and whose locks are hoar,
Yet haste, light skiffs, where myrtle thickets
     smile ;
Love's panthers sleep 'mid roses, as of yore :
"It may be we shall touch the happy isle !"

ENVOY.

Sad eyes ! the blue sea laughs, as heretofore.

Ah, singing birds your happy music pour !

Ah, poets, leave the sordid earth awhile ;

Flit to these ancient gods we still adore :

" It may be we shall touch the happy isle ! "

BALLADE OF THE SUMMER TERM.

(Being a Petition, in the form of a Ballade,
praying the University Commissioners
to spare the Summer Term.)

When Lent and Responsions are ended,
When May with fritillaries waits,
When the flower of the chestnut is splendid,
When drags are at all of the gates
(Those drags the philosopher "slates"
With a scorn that is truly sublime),*
Life wins from the grasp of the Fates
Sweet hours and the fleetest of time!

When wickets are bowl'd and defended,
When Isis is glad with "the Eights,"
When music and sunset are blended,
When Youth and the summer are mates,

---

* Cf. "Suggestions for Academic Reorganization."

When Freshmen are heedless of "Greats,"
And when note-books are cover'd with rhyme,
Ah, these are the hours that one rates —
Sweet hours and the fleetest of time !

When the brow of the Dean is unbended
At luncheons and mild tête-à-têtes,
When the Tutor's in love, nor offended
By blunders in tenses or dates ;
When bouquets are purchased of Bates,
When the bells in their melody chime,
When unheeded the Lecturer prates—
Sweet hours and the fleetest of time !

ENVOY.

Reformers of Schools and of States,
Is mirth so tremendous a crime ?
Ah ! spare what grim pedantry hates—
Sweet hours and the fleetest of time !

BALLADE OF THE MUSE.

Quem tu, Melpomene, semel.

The man whom once, Melpomene,
Thou look'st on with benignant sight,
Shall never at the Isthmus be
A boxer eminent in fight,
Nor fares he foremost in the flight
Of Grecian cars to victory,
Nor goes with Delian laurels dight,
The man thou lov'st, Melpomene!

Not him the Capitol shall see,
As who hath crush'd the threats and might
Of monarchs, march triumphantly;
But Fame shall crown him, in his right
Of all the Roman lyre that smite
The first ; so woods of Tivoli
Proclaim him, so her waters bright,
The man thou lov'st, Melpomene !

The sons of queenly Rome count *me*,
Me too, with them whose chants delight,—
The poets' kindly company ;
Now broken is the tooth of spite,
But thou, that temperest aright
The golden lyre, all, all to thee
He owes—life, fame, and fortune's height—
The man thou lov'st, Melpomene !

ENVOY.

Queen, that to mute lips could'st unite
The wild swan's dying melody !
Thy gifts, ah ! how shall he requite—
The man thou lov'st, Melpomene?

BALLADE AGAINST THE JESUITS.

AFTER LA FONTAINE.

Rome does right well to censure all the vain
Talk of Jansenius, and of them who preach
That earthly joys are damnable! 'Tis plain
We need not charge at Heaven as at a breach;
No, amble on ! We'll gain it, one and all;
The narrow path's a dream fantastical,
And Arnauld's quite superfluously driven
Mirth from the world   We'll scale the
        heavenly wall,
Escobar makes a primrose path to heaven !

He does not hold a man may well be slain
Who vexes with unseasonable speech,
You *may* do murder for five ducats gain,
Not for a pin, a ribbon, or a peach;
He ventures (most consistently) to teach

That there are certain cases that befall
When perjury need no good man appal,
And life of love (he says) may keep a leaven.
Sure, hearing this, a grateful world will bawl,
"Escobar makes a primrose path to heaven!"

" For God's sake read me somewhat in the strain
Of his most cheering volumes, I beseech !"
Why should I name them all ? a mighty train—
So many, none may know the name of each.
Make these your compass to the heavenly beach,
These only in your library instal :
Burn Pascal and his fellows, great and small,
Dolts that in vain with Escobar have striven ;
I tell you, and the common voice doth call,
Escobar makes a primrose path to heaven !

ENVOY.

Satan, that pride did hurry to thy fall,
Thou porter of the grim infernal hall—
Thou keeper of the courts of souls unshriven !
To shun thy shafts, to 'scape thy hellish thrall
Escobar makes a primrose path to heaven !

BALLADE OF DEAD CITIES.

TO E. W. GOSSE.

The dust of Carthage and the dust
Of Babel on the desert wold,
The loves of Corinth, and the lust,
Orchomenos increased with gold ;
The town of Jason, over-bold,
And Cherson, smitten in her prime—
What are they but a dream half-told?
Where are the cities of old time ?

In towns that were a kingdom's trust,
In dim Atlantic forests' fold,
The marble wasteth to a crust,
The granite crumbles into mould ;
O'er these—left nameless from of old—
As over Shinar's brick and slime,
One vast forgetfulness is roll'd—
Where are the cities of old time?

The lapse of ages, and the rust,
The fire, the frost, the waters cold,
Efface the evil and the just ;
From Thebes, that Eriphyle sold,
To drown'd Caer-Is, whose sweet bells toll'd
Beneath the wave a dreamy chime
That echo'd from the mountain-hold,—
"Where are the cities of old time ?"

ENVOY.

Prince, all thy towns and cities must
Decay as these, till all their crime,
And mirth, and wealth, and toil are thrust
Where are the cities of old time.

BALLADE OF THE ROYAL GAME
OF GOLF.

(EAST FIFESHIRE.)

There are laddies will drive ye a ba'
To the burn frae the farthermost tee,
But ye mauna think driving is a',
Ye may heel her, and send her ajee,
Ye may land in the sand or the sea ;
And ye're dune, sir, ye're no worth a preen,
Tak' the word that an auld man 'll gie,
Tak' aye tent to be up on the green !

The auld folk are crouse, and they craw
That their putting is pawky and slee ;
In a bunker they're nae gude ava',
But to girn, and to gar the sand flee.
And a lassie can putt—ony she,—
Be she Maggy, or Bessie, or Jean,

But a cleek-shot's the billy for me,
Tak' aye tent to be up on the green!

I hae play'd in the frost and the thaw,
I hae play'd since the year thirty-three,
I hae play'd in the rain and the snaw,
And I trust I may play till I dee ;
And I tell ye the truth and nae lee,
For I speak o' the thing I hae seen—
Tom Morris, I ken, will agree—
Tak' aye tent to be up on the green !

ENVOY.

Prince, faith you're improving a wee,
And, Lord, man, they tell me you're keen ;
Tak' the best o' advice that can be,
Tak' aye tent to be up on the green !

DOUBLE BALLADE OF PRIMITIVE MAN.

TO J. A. FARRER.

He lived in a cave by the seas,
He lived upon oysters and foes,
But his list of forbidden degrees,
An extensive morality shows ;
Geological evidence goes
To prove he had never a pan,
But he shaved with a shell when he chose,—
'Twas the manner of Primitive Man.

He worshipp'd the rain and the breeze,
He worshipp'd the river that flows,
And the Dawn, and the Moon, and the trees,
And bogies, and serpents, and crows ;
He buried his dead with their toes
Tucked-up, an original plan,
Till their knees came right under their nose, —
'Twas the manner of Primitive Man.

His communal wives, at his ease,
He would curb with occasional blows ;
Or his State had a queen, like the bees
(As another philosopher trows) :
When he spoke, it was never in prose,
But he sang in a strain that would scan,
For (to doubt it, perchance, were morose)
'Twas the manner of Primitive Man !

On the coasts that incessantly freeze,
With his stones, and his bones, and his bows ;
On luxuriant tropical leas,
Where the summer eternally glows,
He is found, and his habits disclose
(Let theology say what she can)
That he lived in the long, long agos,
'Twas the manner of Primitive Man !

From a status like that of the Crees,
Our society's fabric arose,—
Develop'd, evolved, if you please,
But deluded chronologists chose,

In a fancied accordance with Mos
es, 4000 B.C. for the span
When he rushed on the world and its woes,—
'Twas the manner of Primitive Man !

But the mild anthropologist,—*he's*
Not *recent* inclined to suppose
Flints Palæolithic like these,
Quaternary bones such as those !
In Rhinoceros, Mammoth and Co.'s,
First epoch, the Human began,
Theologians all to expose,—
'Tis the *mission* of Primitive Man.

ENVOY.

MAX, proudly your Aryans pose,
But their rigs they undoubtedly ran,
For, as every Darwinian knows,
'Twas the manner of Primitive Man !*

* The last three stanzas are by an eminent Anthropologist.

BALLADE OF AUTUMN.

We built a castle in the air,
In summer weather, you and I,
The wind and sun were in your hair,—
Gold hair against a sapphire sky :
When Autumn came, with leaves that fly
Before the storm, across the plain,
You fled from me, with scarce a sigh—
My Love returns no more again !

The windy lights of Autumn flare :
I watch the moonlit sails go by ;
I marvel how men toil and fare,
The weary business that they ply !
Their voyaging is vanity,
And fairy gold is all their gain,
And all the winds of winter cry,
" My Love returns no more again ! "

Here, in my castle of Despair,
I sit alone with memory ;
The wind-fed wolf has left his lair,
To keep the outcast company.
The brooding owl he hoots hard by,
The hare shall kindle on thy hearth-stane,
The Rhymer's soothest prophecy,—*
My Love returns no more again !

ENVOY.

Lady, my home until I die
Is here, where youth and hope were slain :
They flit, the ghosts of our July,
My Love returns no more again !

* Thomas of Ercildoune.

BALLADE OF TRUE WISDOM.

While others are asking for beauty or fame,
Or praying to know that for which they should
     pray,
Or courting Queen Venus, that affable dame,
Or chasing the Muses the weary and grey,
The sage has found out a more excellent way—
To Pan and to Pallas his incense he showers,
And his humble petition puts up day by day,
For a house full of books, and a garden of flowers.

Inventors may bow to the God that is lame,
And crave from the fire on his stithy a ray ;
Philosophers kneel to the God without name,
Like the people of Athens, agnostics are they ;
The hunter a fawn to Diana will slay,
The maiden wild roses will wreathe for the
     Hours ;
But the wise man will ask, ere libation he pay,
For a house full of books, and a garden of flowers.

Oh ! grant me a life without pleasure or blame

(As mortals count pleasure who rush through
      their day

With a speed to which that of the tempest is
      tame) !

O grant me a house by the beach of a bay,

Where the waves can be surly in winter, and
      play

With the sea-weed in summer, ye bountiful
      powers !

And I'd leave all the hurry, the noise, and the
      fray,

For a house full of books, and a garden of
      flowers.

ENVOY.

Gods, grant or withhold it ; your "yea" and
      your " nay "

Are immutable, heedless of outcry of ours :

But life *is* worth living, and here we would stay

For a house full of books, and a garden of
      flowers.

BALLADE OF WORLDLY WEALTH.

(OLD FRENCH.)

Money taketh town and wall,
Fort and ramp without a blow ;
Money moves the merchants all,
While the tides shall ebb and flow ;
Money maketh Evil show
Like the Good, and Truth like lies :
These alone can ne'er bestow
Youth, and health, and Paradise.

Money maketh festival,
Wine she buys, and beds can strow ;
Round the necks of captains tall,
Money wins them chains to throw,
Marches soldiers to and fro,
Gaineth ladies with sweet eyes :
These alone can ne'er bestow
Youth, and health, and Paradise.

Money wins the priest his stall ;
Money mitres buys, I trow,
Red hats for the Cardinal,
Abbeys for the novice low ;
Money maketh sin as snow,
Place of penitence supplies :
These alone can ne'er bestow
Youth, and health, and Paradise.

BALLADE OF LIFE.

" ' Dead and gone,'—a sorry burden of the Ballad of
  Life."
  Death's Jest Book.

Say, fair maids, maying
In gardens green,
In deep dells straying,
What end hath been
Two Mays between
Of the flowers that shone
And your own sweet queen—
" They are dead and gone ! "

Say, grave priests, praying
In dule and teen,
From cells decaying
What have ye seen
Of the proud and mean,
Of Judas and John,
Of the foul and clean ?—
" They are dead and gone ! "

Say, kings, arraying
Loud wars to win,
Of your manslaying
What gain ye glean?
"They are fierce and keen,
But they fall anon,
On the sword that lean,—
They are dead and gone!"

ENVOY.

Through the mad world's scene,
We are drifting on,
To this tune, I ween,
"They are dead and gone!"

BALLADE OF BLUE CHINA.

There's a joy without canker or cark,
There's a pleasure eternally new,
'Tis to gloat on the glaze and the mark
Of china that's ancient and blue ;
Unchipp'd all the centuries through
It has pass'd, since the chime of it rang,
And they fashion'd it, figure and hue,
In the reign of the Emperor Hwang.

These dragons (their tails, you remark,
Into bunches of gillyflowers grew),—
When Noah came out of the ark,
Did these lie in wait for his crew ?
They snorted, they snapp'd, and they slew,
They were mighty of fin and of fang,
And their portraits Celestials drew
In the reign of the Emperor Hwang.

D

Here's a pot with a cot in a park,
In a park where the peach-blossoms blew,
Where the lovers eloped in the dark,
Lived, died, and were changed into two
Bright birds that eternally flew
Through the boughs of the may, as they sang ;
'Tis a tale was undoubtedly true
In the reign of the Emperor Hwang.

ENVOY.

Come, snarl at my ecstasies, do,
Kind critic, your " tongue has a tang "
But—a sage never heeded a shrew
In the reign of the Emperor Hwang.

BALLADE OF DEAD LADIES.

(AFTER VILLON.)

Nay, tell me now in what strange air
The Roman Flora dwells to-day.
Where Archippiada hides, and where
Beautiful Thais has passed away?
Whence answers Echo, afield, astray,
By mere or stream,—around, below?
Lovelier she than a woman of clay;
Nay, but where is the last year's snow?

Where is wise Héloïse, that care
Brought on Abeilard, and dismay?
All for her love he found a snare,
A maimed poor monk in orders grey;
And where's the Queen who willed to slay
Buridan, that in a sack must go
Afloat down Seine,—a perilous way—
Nay, but where is the last year's snow?

Where's that White Queen, a lily rare,
With her sweet song, the Siren's lay?
Where's Bertha Broad-foot, Beatrice fair?
Alys and Ermengarde, where are they?
Good Joan, whom English did betray
In Rouen town, and burned her? No,
Maiden and Queen, no man may say;
Nay, but where is the last year's snow?

ENVOY.

Prince, all this week thou need'st not pray,
Nor yet this year the thing to know.
One burden answers, ever and aye,
"Nay, but where is the last year's snow?"

VILLON'S BALLADE

OF GOOD COUNSEL, TO HIS FRIENDS OF EVIL LIFE.

Nay, be you pardoner or cheat,
Or cogger keen, or mumper shy,
You'll burn your fingers at the feat,
And howl like other folks that fry.
All evil folks that love a lie !
And where goes gain that greed amasses,
By wile, and trick, and thievery ?
'Tis all to taverns and to lasses !

Rhyme, rail, dance, play the cymbals sweet,
With game, and shame, and jollity,
Go jigging through the field and street,
With *myst'ry* and *morality ;*
Win gold at *gleek,*—and that will fly,
Where all you gain at *passage* passes,—
And that's ? You know as well as I,
'Tis all to taverns and to lasses !

Nay, forth from all such filth retreat,
Go delve and ditch, in wet or dry,
Turn groom, give horse and mule their meat,
If you've no clerkly skill to ply ;
You'll gain enough, with husbandry,
But—sow hempseed and such wild grasses,
And where goes all you take thereby?—
'Tis all to taverns and to lasses !

ENVOY.

Your clothes, your hose, your broidery,
Your linen that the snow surpasses,
Or ere they're worn, off, off they fly,
'Tis all to taverns and to lasses !

BALLADE OF THE BOOKWORM.

Far in the Past I peer, and see
A Child upon the Nursery floor,
A Child with books upon his knee,
Who asks, like Oliver, for more !
The number of his years is IV,
And yet in Letters hath he skill,
How deep he dives in Fairy-lore !
The Books I loved, I love them still !

One gift the Fairies gave me : (Three
They commonly bestowed of yore)
The Love of Books, the Golden Key
That opens the Enchanted Door :
Behind it BLUEBEARD lurks, and o'er
And o'er doth JACK his Giants kill,
And there is all ALADDIN'S store,—
The Books I loved, I love them still !

Take all, but leave my Books to me !

These heavy creels of old we bore

We fill not now, nor wander free,

Nor wear the heart that once we wore ;

Not now each River seems to pour

His waters from the Muses' hill ;

Though something's gone from stream and
        shore,

The Books I loved, I love them still !

ENVOY.

Fate, that art Queen by shore and sea,

We bow submissive to thy will,

Ah grant, by some benign decree,

The Books I loved—to love them still.

VALENTINE IN FORM OF BALLADE.

The soft wind from the south land sped,
He set his strength to blow,
From forests where Adonis bled,
And lily flowers a-row :
He crossed the straits like streams that flow,
The ocean dark as wine,
To my true love to whisper low,
To be your Valentine.

The Spring half-raised her drowsy head,
Besprent with drifted snow,
" I'll send an April day," she said,
" To lands of wintry woe."
He came,—the winter's overthrow
With showers that sing and shine,
Pied daisies round your path to strow,
To be your Valentine.

Where sands of Egypt, swart and red,
'Neath suns Egyptian glow,
In places of the princely dead,
By the Nile's overflow,
The swallow preened her wings to go,
And for the North did pine,
And fain would brave the frost her foe,
To be your Valentine.

ENVOY.

Spring, Swallow, South Wind, even so,
Their various voice combine ;
But that they crave on *me* bestow,
To be your Valentine.

BALLADE OF OLD PLAYS.

(Les Œuvres de Monsieur Molière. A Paris,
chez Louys Billaine, à la Palme.
M.D.C.LXVI.)

LA COUR.

When these Old Plays were new, the King,
Beside the Cardinal's chair,
Applauded, 'mid the courtly ring,
The verses of Molière ;
Point-lace was then the only wear,
Old Corneille came to woo,
And bright Du Parc was young and fair,
When these Old Plays were new !

LA COMÉDIE.

How shrill the butcher's cat-calls ring,
How loud the lackeys swear !
Black pipe-bowls on the stage they fling,
At Brécourt, fuming there !

The Porter 's stabbed ! a Mousquetaire
Breaks in with noisy crew—
'Twas all a commonplace affair
When these Old Plays were new !

LA VILLE.

When these Old Plays were new ! They bring
A host of phantoms rare :
Old jests that float, old jibes that sting,
Old faces peaked with care :
Ménage's smirk, de Visé's stare,
The thefts of Jean Ribou,—*
Ah, publishers were hard to bear
When these Old Plays were new.

ENVOY.

Ghosts, at your Poet's word ye dare
To break Death's dungeons through,
And frisk, as in that golden air,
When these Old Plays were new !

* A knavish publisher.

BALLADE OF HIS BOOKS.

Here stand my books, line upon line
They reach the roof, and row by row,
They speak of faded tastes of mine,
And things I did, but do not, know :
Old school books, useless long ago,
Old Logics, where the spirit, railed in,
Could scarcely answer " yes " or " no "—
The many things I've tried and failed in !

Here's Villon, in morocco fine,
(The Poet starved, in mud and snow,)
Glatigny does not crave to dine,
And René's tears forget to flow.
And here's a work by Mrs. Crowe,
With hosts of ghosts and bogies jailed in ;
Ah, all my ghosts have gone below—
The many things I've tried and failed in !

He's touched, this mouldy Greek divine,
The Princess D'Este's hand of snow ;
And here the arms of D'Hoym shine,
And there's a tear-bestained Rousseau :
Here's Carlyle shrieking "woe on woe"
(The first edition, this, he wailed in) ;
I once believed in him—but oh,
The many things I've tried and failed in !

ENVOY.

Prince, tastes may differ ; mine and thine
Quite other balances are scaled in ;
May you succeed, though I repine—
"The many things I've tried and failed in !"

BALLADE OF THE DREAM.

Swift as sound of music fled
When no more the organ sighs,
Sped as all old days are sped,
So your lips, love, and your eyes,
So your gentle-voiced replies
Mine one hour in sleep that seem,
Rise and flit when slumber flies,
Following darkness like a dream!

Like the scent from roses red,
Like the dawn from golden skies,
Like the semblance of the dead
From the living love that hies,
Like the shifting shade that lies
On the moonlight-silvered stream,
So you rise when dreams arise,
Following darkness like a dream!

Could some spell, or sung or said,
Could some kindly witch and wise,
Lull for aye this dreaming head
In a mist of memories,
I would lie like him who lies
Where the lights on Latmos gleam,—
Wake not, find not Paradise
Following darkness like a dream !

ENVOY.

Sleep, that giv'st what Life denies,
Shadowy bounties and supreme,
Bring the dearest face that flies
Following darkness like a dream !

BALLADE OF THE SOUTHERN
CROSS.

Fair islands of the silver fleece,
Hoards of unsunned, uncounted gold,
Whose havens are the haunts of Peace,
Whose boys are in our quarrel bold;
Our bolt is shot, our tale is told,
Our ship of state in storms may toss,
But ye are young if we are old,
Ye Islands of the Southern Cross!

Ay, *we* must dwindle and decrease,
Such fates the ruthless years unfold;
And yet we shall not wholly cease,
We shall not perish unconsoled;
Nay, still shall Freedom keep her hold
Within the sea's inviolate fosse,
And boast her sons of English mould,
Ye Islands of the Southern Cross!

E

All empires tumble—Rome and Greece—
Their swords are rust, their altars cold !
For us, the Children of the Seas,
Who ruled where'er the waves have rolled,
For us, in Fortune's books enscrolled,
I read no runes of hopeless loss ;
Nor—while *ye* last—our knell is tolled,
Ye Islands of the Southern Cross !

ENVOY.

Britannia, when thy hearth's a-cold,
When o'er thy grave has grown the moss,
Still *Rule Australia* shall be trolled
In Islands of the Southern Cross !

BALLADE OF AUCASSIN

Where smooth the southern waters run
By rustling leagues of poplars grey,
Beneath a veiled soft southern sun,
We wandered out of yesterday,
Went maying through that ancient May
Whose fallen flowers are fragrant yet,
And loitered by the fountain spray
With Aucassin and Nicolette.

The grass-grown paths are trod of none
Where through the woods they went astray.
The spider's traceries are spun
Across the darkling forest way.
There come no knights that ride to slay,
No pilgrims through the grasses wet,
No shepherd lads that sang their say
With Aucassin and Nicolette!

'Twas here by Nicolette begun
Her bower of boughs and grasses gay ;
'Scaped from the cell of marble dun
'Twas here the lover found the fay,
Ah, lovers fond ! ah, foolish play !
How hard we find it to forget
Who fain would dwell with them as they,
With Aucassin and Nicolette.

ENVOY.

Prince, 'tis a melancholy lay !
For youth, for love we both regret.
How fair they seem, how far away,
With Aucassin and Nicolette !

BALLADE AMOUREUSE.

AFTER FROISSART.

Not Jason nor Medea wise,
I crave to see, nor win much lore,
Nor list to Orpheus' minstrelsies ;
Nor Her'cles would I see, that o'er
The wide world roamed from shore to shore ;
Nor, by St. James, Penelope,—
Nor pure Lucrece, such wrong that bore :
To see my Love suffices me !

Virgil and Cato, no man vies
With them in wealth of clerkly store ;
I would not see them with mine eyes ;
Nor him that sailed, *sans* sail nor oar,
Across the barren sea and hoar,
And all for love of his ladye ;
Nor pearl nor sapphire takes me more :
To see my Love suffices me !

I heed not Pegasus, that flies
As swift as shafts the bowmen pour ;
Nor famed Pygmalion's artifice,
Whereof the like was ne'er before ;
Nor Oléus, that drank of yore
The salt wave of the whole great sea :
Why ? dost thou ask ? 'Tis as I swore—
To see my Love suffices me !

BALLADE OF QUEEN ANNE.

The modish Airs,
The Tansey Brew,
The *Swains* and *Fairs*
In curtained Pew;
Nymphs KNELLER drew,
Books BENTLEY read,—
Who knows them, who?
QUEEN ANNE is dead!

We buy her Chairs,
Her China blue,
Her red-brick Squares
We build anew;
But ah! we rue,
When all is said,
The tale o'er-true,
QUEEN ANNE is dead!

Now *Bulls* and *Bears*,
A ruffling Crew,
With Stocks and Shares,
With Turk and Jew,
Go bubbling through
The Town ill-bred :   '
The World's askew,
QUEEN ANNE is dead !

ENVOY.

Friend, praise the new ;
The old is fled :
Vivat FROU-FROU !
QUEEN ANNE is dead !

BALLADE OF BLIND LOVE.

(AFTER LYONNET DE COISMES.)

Who have loved and ceased to love, forget
That ever they loved in their lives, they say ;
Only remember the fever and fret,
And the pain of Love, that was all his pay ;
All the delight of him passes away
From hearts that hoped, and from lips that
     met—
Too late did I love you, my love, and yet
I shall never forget till my dying day.

Too late were we 'ware of the secret net
That meshes the feet in the flowers that stray ;
There were we taken and snared, Lisette,
In the dungeon of 𝕷𝖆 𝕱𝖆𝖚𝖘𝖘𝖊 𝕬𝖒𝖎𝖘𝖙𝖎𝖊 ;
Help was there none in the wide world's fray,
Joy was there none in the gift and the debt ;

Too late we knew it, too long regret—
I shall never forget till my dying day !

We must live our lives, though the sun be set,
Must meet in the masque where parts we play,
Must cross in the maze of Life's minuet ;
Our yea is yea, and our nay is nay :
But while snows of winter or flowers of May
Are the sad year's shroud or coronet,
In the season of rose or of violet,
I shall never forget till my dying day !

ENVOY.

Queen, when the clay is my coverlet,
When I am dead, and when you are grey,
Vow, where the grass of the grave is wet,
" I shall never forget till my dying day !"

BALLADE OF HIS CHOICE OF A SEPULCHRE.

Here I'd come when weariest !
    Here the breast
Of the Windburg's tufted over
Deep with bracken ; here his crest
    Takes the west,
Where the wide-winged hawk doth hover.

Silent here are lark and plover ;
    In the cover
Deep below the cushat best
Loves his mate, and croons above her
    O'er their nest,
Where the wide-winged hawk doth hover.

Bring me here, Life's tired-out guest,
    To the blest
Bed that waits the weary rover,

Here should failure be confessed;
  Ends my quest,
Where the wide-winged hawk doth hover!

ENVOY.

Friend, or stranger kind, or lover,
Ah, fulfil a last behest,
  Let me rest
Where the wide-winged hawk doth hover!

DIZAIN.

As, to the pipe, with rhythmic feet
In windings of some old-world dance,
The smiling couples cross and meet,
Join hands, and then in line advance,
So, to these fair old tunes of France,
Through all their maze of to-and-fro,
The light-heeled numbers laughing go,
Retreat, return, and ere they flee,
One moment pause in panting row,
*And seem to say—*Vos plaudite !

A. D.

VERSES AND TRANSLATIONS.

ORONTE—*Ce ne sont point de ces grands vers pompeux,*
Mais de petits vers!

"Le Misanthrope," Acte i., Sc. 2.

A PORTRAIT OF 1783.

Your hair and chin are like the hair
And chin Burne-Jones's ladies wear;
You were unfashionably fair
    In '83;
And sad you were when girls are gay,
You read a book about *Le vrai*
Mérite de l'homme, alone in May.

    What *can* it be,
Le vrai mérite de l'homme? Not gold,
Not titles that are bought and sold,
Not wit that flashes and is cold,
    But Virtue merely!
Instructed by Jean-Jacques Rousseau
(And Jean-Jacques, surely, ought to know),
You bade the crowd of foplings go,
    You glanced severely,

F

Dreaming beneath the spreading shade
Of ' that vast hat the Graces made ; ' *
So Rouget sang—while yet he played
    With courtly rhyme,
And hymned great Doisi's red perruque,
And Nice's eyes, and Zulmé's look,
And dead canaries, ere he shook
    The sultry time

With strains like thunder.   Loud and low
Methinks I hear the murmur grow,
The tramp of men that come and go
    With fire and sword.
They war against the quick and dead,
Their flying feet are dashed with red,
As theirs the vintaging that tread
    Before the Lord.

---

   * Vous y verrez, belle Julie,
     Que ce chapeau tout maltraité
     Fut, dans un instant de folie,
     Par les Grâces même inventé.

'À Julie.'   *Essais en Prose et en Vers*, par Joseph
   Lisle ; Paris. An. V. de la République.

O head unfashionably fair,

What end was thine, for all thy care?

We only see thee dreaming there :

     We cannot see

The breaking of thy vision, when

The Rights of Man were lords of men,

When virtue won her own again

     In '93.

THE MOON'S MINION.

(FROM THE PROSE OF C. BAUDELAIRE.)

Thine eyes are like the sea, my dear,
   The wand'ring waters, green and grey;
Thine eyes are wonderful and clear,
   And deep, and deadly, even as they;
The spirit of the changeful sea
   Informs thine eyes at night and noon,
She sways the tides, and the heart of thee,
   The mystic, sad, capricious Moon!

The Moon came down the shining stair
   Of clouds that fleck the summer sky,
She kissed thee, saying, " Child, be fair,
   And madden men's hearts, even as I;
Thou shalt love all things strange and sweet,
   That know me and are known of me;
The lover thou shalt never meet,
   The land where thou shalt never be!"

She held thee in her chill embrace,
   She kissed thee with cold lips divine,
She left her pallor on thy face,
   That mystic ivory face of thine ;
And now I sit beside thy feet,
   And all my heart is far from thee,
Dreaming of her I shall not meet,
   And of the land I shall not see !

IN ITHACA.

"And now am I greatly repenting that ever I left my
life with thee, and the immortality thou didst promise
me."—*Letter of Odysseus to Calypso.* Luciani *Vera
Historia.*

'Tis thought Odysseus when the strife was o'er
    With all the waves and wars, a weary while,
    Grew restless in his disenchanted isle,
And still would watch the sunset, from the
        shore,
Go down the ways of gold, and evermore
    His sad heart followed after, mile on mile,
    Back to the Goddess of the magic wile,
Calypso, and the love that was of yore.

Thou too, thy haven gained, must turn thee yet
    To look across the sad and stormy space,
    Years of a youth as bitter as the sea,
Ah, with a heavy heart, and eyelids wet,
    Because, within a fair forsaken place
    The life that might have been is lost to thee.

HOMER.

Homer, thy song men liken to the sea
   With all the notes of music in its tone,
   With tides that wash the dim dominion
Of Hades, and light waves that laugh in glee
Around the isles enchanted ; nay, to me
    Thy verse seems as the River of source
      unknown
    That glasses Egypt's temples overthrown
In his sky-nurtured stream, eternally.

No wiser we than men of heretofore
   To find thy sacred fountains guarded fast ;
Enough, thy flood makes green our human
    shore,
    As Nilus Egypt, rolling down his vast
His fertile flood, that murmurs evermore
   Of gods dethroned, and empires in the past.

THE BURIAL OF MOLIÈRE.

(AFTER J. TRUFFIER.)

Dead—he is dead ! The rouge has left a trace
　　On that thin cheek where shone, perchance,
　　　　a tear,
　　Even while the people laughed that held
　　　　him dear
But yesterday.   He died,—and not in grace,
And many a black-robed caitiff starts apace
　　To slander him whose *Tartuffe* made them
　　　　fear,
　　And gold must win a passage for his bier,
And bribe the crowd that guards his resting-
　　　　place.

Ah, Molière, for that last time of all,
　　Man's hatred broke upon thee, and went by,
And did but make more fair thy funeral.
　　Though in the dark they hid thee stealthily,
Thy coffin had the cope of night for pall,
　　For torch, the stars along the windy sky !

BION.

The wail of Moschus on the mountains crying
  The Muses heard, and loved it long ago ;
They heard the hollows of the hills replying,
  They heard the weeping water's overflow ;
They winged the sacred strain—the song
      undying,
  The song that all about the world must go,—
When poets for a poet dead are sighing,
  The minstrels for a minstrel friend laid low.

And dirge to dirge that answers, and the
      weeping
  For Adonais by the summer sea,
The plaints for Lycidas, and Thyrsis (sleeping
  Far from 'the forest ground called Thessaly'),
These hold thy memory, Bion, in their keeping,
  And are but echoes of the moan for thee.

SPRING.

(AFTER MELEAGER.)

Now the bright crocus flames, and now
  The slim narcissus takes the rain,
And, straying o'er the mountain's brow,
  The daffodilies bud again.
  The thousand blossoms wax and wane
On wold, and heath, and fragrant bough,
But fairer than the flowers art thou,
  Than any growth of hill or plain.

Ye gardens, cast your leafy crown,
That my Love's feet may tread it down,
  Like lilies on the lilies set ;
My Love, whose lips are softer far
Than drowsy poppy petals are,
  And sweeter than the violet !

BEFORE THE SNOW.

(AFTER ALBERT GLATIGNY.)

The winter is upon us, not the snow,
   The hills are etched on the horizon bare,
   The skies are iron grey, a bitter air,
The meagre cloudlets shudder to and fro.
One yellow leaf the listless wind doth blow,
   Like some strange butterfly, unclassed and
      rare.
   Your footsteps ring in frozen alleys, where
The black trees seem to shiver as you go.

Beyond lie church and steeple, with their old
   And rusty vanes that rattle as they veer,
A sharper gust would shake them from their
      hold,
   Yet up that path, in summer of the year,
And past that melancholy pile we strolled
   To pluck wild strawberries, with merry cheer.

VILLANELLE.

TO LUCIA.

Apollo left the golden Muse
  And shepherded a mortal's sheep,
Theocritus of Syracuse!

To mock the giant swain that woo's
  The sea-nymph in the sunny deep,
Apollo left the golden Muse.

Afield he drove his lambs and ewes,
  Where Milon and where Battus reap,
Theocritus of Syracuse !

To watch thy tunny-fishers cruise
  Below the dim Sicilian steep
Apollo left the golden Muse.

Ye twain did loiter in the dews,
  Ye slept the swain's unfever'd sleep,
Theocritus of Syracuse !

That Time might half with *his* confuse
    Thy songs,—like his, that laugh and leap,—
Theocritus of Syracuse,
    Apollo left the golden Muse !

NATURAL THEOLOGY.

ἐπεὶ καὶ τοῦτον ὀίομαι ἀθανάτοισιν
ἐυχέσθαι· Πάντες δὲ θεῶν χατέουσ᾽ ἄνθρωποι.
                                    OD. III. 47.

" Once CAGN was like a father, kind and good,
    But He was spoiled by fighting many things;
He wars upon the lions in the wood,
    And breaks the Thunder-bird's tremendous
        wings ;
But still we cry to Him,— *We are thy brood*—
    O *Cagn, be merciful!* and us He brings
To herds of elands, and great store of food,
    And in the desert opens water-springs."

So Qing, King Nqsha's Bushman hunter, spoke,
    Beside the camp-fire, by the fountain fair,

When all were weary, and soft clouds of smoke
  Were fading, fragrant, in the twilit air :
And suddenly in each man's heart there woke
  A pang, a sacred memory of prayer.

THE ODYSSEY.

As one that for a weary space has lain
　　Lulled by the song of Circe and her wine
　　In gardens near the pale of Proserpine,
Where that Ææan isle forgets the main,
And only the low lutes of love complain,
　　And only shadows of wan lovers pine,
　　As such an one were glad to know the brine
Salt on his lips, and the large air again,—
So gladly, from the songs of modern speech
　　Men turn, and see the stars, and feel the free
　　　　Shrill wind beyond the close of heavy
　　　　　　flowers,
　　　　And through the music of the languid
　　　　　　hours,
They hear like ocean on a western beach
　　The surge and thunder of the Odyssey.

IDEAL.

*Suggested by a female head in wax, of unknown
date, but supposed to be either of the best Greek
age, or a work of Raphael or Leonardo. It is
now in the Lille Museum.*

Ah, mystic child of Beauty, nameless maid,
    Dateless and fatherless, how long ago,
A Greek, with some rare sadness overweighed,
    Shaped thee, perchance, and quite forgot his
        woe !
    Or Raphael thy sweetness did bestow,
While magical his fingers o'er thee strayed,
    Or that great pupil taught of Verrocchio
Redeemed thy still perfection from the shade

That hides all fair things lost, and things
        unborn,
    Where one has fled from me, that wore thy
        grace,

G

And that grave tenderness of thine awhile ;
Nay, still in dreams I see her, but her face
Is pale, is wasted with a touch of scorn,
And only on thy lips I find her smile.

THE FAIRY'S GIFT.

"Take short views."—SYDNEY SMITH.

The Fays that to my christ'ning came
   (For come they did, my nurses taught me),
They did not bring me wealth or fame,
   'Tis very little that they brought me.
But one, the crossest of the crew,
   The ugly old one, uninvited,
Said, " I shall be avenged on *you*,
   My child; you shall grow up short-sighted !"
With magic juices did she lave
   Mine eyes, and wrought her wicked pleasure.
Well, of all gifts the Fairies gave,
   Hers is the present that I treasure !

The bore whom others fear and flee,
   I do not fear, I do not flee him ;
I pass him calm as calm can be ;
   I do not cut—I do not see him !

And with my feeble eyes and dim,
  Where *you* see patchy fields and fences,
For me the mists of Turner swim—
  My "azure distance" soon commences !
Nay, as I blink about the streets
  Of this befogged and miry city,
Why, almost every girl one meets
  Seems preternaturally pretty !
"Try spectacles," one's friends intone ;
  "You'll see the world correctly through
      them."
But I have visions of my own,
  And not for worlds would I undo them !

BENEDETTA RAMUS.

AFTER ROMNEY.

Mysterious Benedetta ! who
That Reynolds or that Romney drew
Was ever half so fair as you,
 Or is so well forgot ?
These eyes of melancholy brown,
These woven locks, a shadowy crown,
Must surely have bewitched the town ;
 Yet you're remembered not.

Through all that prattle of your age,
Through lore of fribble and of sage
I've read, and chiefly Walpole's page,
 Wherein are beauties famous ;
I've haunted ball, and rout, and sale :
I've heard of Devonshire and Thrale,
And all the Gunnings' wondrous tale,
 But nothing of Miss Ramus.

And yet on many a lattice pane
'Fair Benedetta,' scrawled in vain
By lovers' diamonds, must remain
   To tell us you were cruel.*
But who, of all that sighed and swore—
Wits, poets, courtiers by the score—
Did win and on his bosom wore
   This hard and lovely jewel?

Why, dilettante records say
An Alderman, who came that way,
Woo'd you and made you Lady Day;
   You crowned his civic flame.
It suits a melancholy song
To think your heart had suffered wrong,
And that you lived not very long
   To be a City dame !

Perchance you were a Mourning Bride,
And conscious of a heart that died

---

* "I have broken many a pane of glass marked Cruel
Parthenissa," says the aunt of Sophia Western in *Tom
Jones.*

With one who fell by Rodney's side
  In blood-stained Spanish bays.
Perchance 'twas no such thing, and you
Dwelt happy with your knight and true,
And, like Aurora, watched a crew
  Of rosy little Days !

Oh, lovely face and innocent !
Whatever way your fortunes went,
And if to earth your life was lent
  For little space or long,
In your kind eyes we seem to see
What Woman at her best may be,
And offer to your memory
  An unavailing song !

PARTANT POUR LA SCRIBIE.

[Scribie, on the north-east littoral of Bohemia, is the
land of stage conventions.   It is named after the dis-
coverer, M. Scribe.]

A pleasant land is Scribie, where
    The light comes mostly from below,
And seems a sort of symbol rare
    Of things at large, and how they go,
In rooms where doors are everywhere
    And cupboards shelter friend or foe.

This is a realm where people tell
    Each other, when they chance to meet,
Of things that long ago befell—
    And do most solemnly repeat
Secrets they both know very well,
    Aloud, and in the public street !

A land where lovers go in fours,
    Master and mistress, man and maid ;

Where people listen at the doors
    Or 'neath a table's friendly shade,
And comic Irishmen in scores
    Roam o'er the scenes all undismayed :

A land where Virtue in distress
    Owes much to uncles in disguise ;
Where British sailors frankly bless
    Their limbs, their timbers, and their eyes ;
And where the villain doth confess,
    Conveniently, before he dies !

A land of lovers false and gay ;
    A land where people dread a " curse ; "
A land of letters gone astray,
    Or intercepted, which is worse ;
Where weddings false fond maids betray,
    And all the babes are changed at nurse.

Oh, happy land, where things come right !
    We of the world where things go ill ;
Where lovers love, but don't unite ;
    Where no one finds the Missing Will—
Dominion of the heart's delight,
    Scribie, we've loved, and love thee still !

ST. ANDREW'S BAY.

NIGHT.

Ah, listen through the music, from the shore,
The " melancholy long-withdrawing roar ";
Beneath the Minster, and the windy caves,
The wide North Ocean, marshalling his waves!
Even so forlorn—in worlds beyond our ken—
May sigh the seas that are not heard of men ;
Even so forlorn, prophetic of man's fate,
Sounded the cold sea-wave disconsolate,
When none but God might hear the boding tone,
As God shall hear the long lament alone,
When all is done, when all the tale is told,
And the gray sea-wave echoes as of old !

MORNING.

This was the burden of the Night,
    The saying of the sea,

But lo ! the hours have brought the light,
The laughter of the waves, the flight
Of dipping sea-birds, foamy white,
    That are so glad to be !
" Forget ! " the happy creatures cry,
    " Forget Night's monotone,
With us be glad in sea and sky,
The days are thine, the days that fly,
The days God gives to know him by,
    And not the Night alone ! "

WOMAN AND THE WEED.

(FOUNDED ON A NEW ZEALAND MYTH.)

In the Morning of Time, when his fortunes
    began,
How bleak, how un-Greek, was the Nature of
    Man !
From his wigwam, if ever he ventured to roam,
There was nobody waiting to welcome him
    home ;
For the Man had been made, but the woman
    had *not*,
And Earth was a highly detestable spot.
Man hated his neighbours; they met and they
    scowled,
They did not converse but they struggled and
    howled,

For Man had no tact—he would ne'er take a
    hint,
And his notions he backed with a hatchet of
    flint.

So Man was alone, and he wished he could see
On the Earth some one like him, but fairer than
    he,
With locks like the red gold, a smile like the
    sun,
To welcome him back when his hunting was
    done.
And he sighed for a voice that should answer
    him still,
Like the affable Echo he heard on the hill :
That should answer him softly and always agree,
And oh, Man reflected, *how nice it would be!*

So he prayed to the Gods, and they stooped to
    his prayer,
And they spoke to the Sun on his way through
    the air,
And he married the Echo one fortunate morn,

And Woman, their beautiful daughter, was
    born !
The daughter of Sunshine and Echo she came
With a voice like a song, with a face like a
    flame ;
With a face like a flame, and a voice like a
    song,
And happy was Man, but it was not for long !

For weather's a painfully changeable thing,
Not always the child of the Echo would sing ;
And the face of the Sun may be hidden with
    mist,
And his child can be terribly cross if she list.
And unfortunate Man had to learn with surprise
That a frown's not peculiar to masculine eyes ;
That the sweetest of voices can scold and can
    sneer,
And cannot be answered—like men—with a
    spear.

So Man went and called to the Gods in his woe,
And they answered him—" Sir, you would
    needs have it so ;

And the thing must go on as the thing has
  begun,

She's immortal—your child of the Echo and
  Sun.

But we'll send you another, and fairer is she,

This maiden with locks that are flowing and
  free.

This maiden so gentle, so kind, and so fair,

With a flower like a star in the night of her
  hair.

With her eyes like the smoke that is misty and
  blue,

With her heart that is heavenly, and tender,
  and true.

She will die in the night, but no need you
  should mourn,

You shall bury her body and thence shall be
  born

A weed that is green, that is fragrant and
  fair,

With a flower like the star in the night of her
  hair.

And the leaves must ye burn till they offer to
  you

Soft smoke, like her eyes that are misty and
    blue.

" And the smoke shall ye breathe and no more
    shall ye fret,
But the child of the Echo and Sun shall forget :
Shall forget all the trouble and torment she
    brings,
Shall bethink ye of none but delectable things ;
And the sound of the wars with your brethren
    shall cease,
While ye smoke by the camp-fire the great pipe
    of peace."
So the last state of Man was by no means the
    worst,
The second gift softened the sting of the first.

Nor the child of the Echo and Sun doth he
    heed
When he dreams with the Maid that was
    changed to the weed ;
Though the Echo be silent, the Sun in a mist,
The Maid is the fairest that ever was kissed.

And when tempests are over and ended the
    rain,
And the child of the Sunshine is sunny again,
He comes back, glad at heart, and again is at
    one
With the changeable child of the Echo and
    Sun.

THE END.

CHISWICK PRESS :—CHARLES WHITTINGHAM AND CO.
TOOKS COURT, CHANCERY LANE.

www.ingramcontent.com/pod-product-compliance
Lightning Source LLC
Chambersburg PA
CBHW020801020726
47495CB00008B/2534